Etta the Elephant Fairy

Join the Rainbow Magic Reading Challenge!

Read the story and collect your fairy points to climb the Reading Rainbow at the back of the book.

To Emily, who loves the elephant kingdom

Special thanks to

Karen Ball

ORCHARD BOOKS

First published in Great Britain in 2018 by The Watts Publishing Group

1 3 5 7 9 10 8 6 4 2

A CIP catalogue record for this book is available from the British Library.

ISBN 978 1 40835 500 8

Printed and bound in Great Britain by CPI Group (UK) Ltd, Croydon, CR0 4YY

The pape … sources

Etta the Elephant Fairy

by Daisy Meadows

www.rainbowmagicbooks.co.uk

Fairyland Palace

Sparkle Forest

Snow Leopard Enclosure

The Girls' Cabin

Elephant Bath

TAIL AND TRUNK SAFARI PARK

Jack Frost's Ice Castle
Blue Ice Mountains
Giraffe Junction
POLAR ZONE
The Polar Bear Enclosure
Cheeky Chimp Corner
TAIL AND TRUNK SAFARI PARK

Jack Frost's Spell

I want a zoo – don't say I'm wrong!
But finding pets takes far too long.
Fill each cage with stinky straw.
I will get what I'm wishing for!

In Sparkle Forest every day,
Peculiar creatures run and play.
The animals are rare – so what?
Get in there and steal the lot!

Contents

Chapter One
The Tiger Stripe Ride

Rachel Walker gazed out of the car window as they turned into the gates of Tail and Trunk Safari Park, on the edge of Wetherbury Village. "Wow, I can't believe we're here!"

"I'm so glad we entered the competition," Kirsty Tate said, sitting beside her friend.

At school, Rachel had made a collage of all the endangered animals in the world, including tigers and pandas and even a tiny Amazonian frog. Rachel's teacher had entered her collage for a picture competition run by the safari park – and she'd won!

The prize was a trip to the park, with Rachel's parents. They were going to learn all about how to help animals

and save them from danger. Best of all, they were booked to stay in a cabin overnight!

The car bumped down the drive, past a gift shop and into the park.

"There's the monkey enclosure!" Rachel said, pointing towards a cluster of trees where monkeys swung by their long tails.

"And that's the Giraffe Junction," Kirsty said, gazing up and up and up at the long neck of a giraffe chewing leaves. The giraffe flicked an ear at them and they laughed

with delight.

"And this looks like our home for the night," said Mrs Walker, as they pulled up outside a cabin. There were red and white gingham curtains at the windows and a banner above the door that read 'WELCOME, RACHEL AND KIRSTY'! The girls shared an excited glance as they clambered out of the car.

The park manager was standing in front of the cabin, waiting for them. "I'm Ahmed," he said, reaching out to shake their hands. "If you leave your bags here, I'll show you round the rest of the park."

Kirsty and Rachel handed over their bags to Mr and Mrs Walker, who

grinned. "We'll unpack. You girls go and have fun. Report back on all the animals!"

Ahmed led the girls over to a truck painted in tiger stripes of orange and black, with big wheels and orange hubs. "I've worked here all my life," he told them, gazing proudly across the grassland. "You're in for a treat!"

Kirsty and Rachel clambered into the back seat and Ahmed switched the engine on. "Ready?"

"Ready!" Rachel and Kirsty replied, clapping their hands together in delight.

The safari park was HUGE. Ahmed turned the truck through a gate and drove slowly past a big, open lake that glittered in the sunshine.

Honk! HONK!

"What's that noise?" Rachel asked, looking round.

Kirsty spotted a pair of wet, shiny noses poking above the surface of the water. "Seals!" she said.

The truck entered a copse of trees and bamboo, and the girls saw a panda lazing in a branch, chewing a twig. His

soft, black eyes watched them as they drove past.

"I love pandas!" Rachel whispered.

"And there – look." Kirsty pointed at a huge rhinoceros that was bathing in a puddle of mud. He lazily scratched one ear on a tree stump.

"The mud keeps him cool in the sun," Ahmed said. "Did you know that the word 'rhinoceros' means 'nose horn'?"

"No, we didn't," Rachel and Kirsty said, smiling at each other. Ahmed told them all about how many species of rhinos

there were, and that they could grow to over four metres long. He definitely loved his animal facts.

There was so much to see! Eventually, the truck arrived back at their cabin.

"Would you like to visit the Elephant Bath later?" Ahmed asked, turning round from the driver's seat. "The elephants are sleeping now but they'll come out at dusk, when it's cooler."

"Yes, please!" the girls said together.

"We can go after supper," Ahmed said,

and drove off in a cloud of dust.

Rachel and Kirsty waved goodbye, then ran into the cabin.

"I'm not sure I'm going to be able to sleep tonight," Rachel said, as she placed her toothbrush in a glass on the sink.

"Me neither," said Kirsty.

The cabin was so cute – above Kirsty's bed, there was a little shelf filled with miniature felt stuffed animals, including a little elephant. As they looked at it, it began to glow.

Kirsty and Rachel linked hands and drew closer. Rachel's heart was fluttering. She knew exactly what this meant – one of their fairy friends was coming to visit them. No matter how many fairies they met, each one was special. And as they spotted a cloud of silver glitter, this one looked more special than ever!

Chapter Two
Glade Creatures

A fairy flew out from behind the little felt elephant.

"Hello, Kirsty and Rachel," she said, in a voice that tinkled like a bell. "I'm Etta the Elephant Fairy." She was wearing a pair of yellow culottes and a white top with a leaf pattern. The fairy floated over to them through the air.

"Hello, Etta," they said brightly.

"I'm so glad you're here!" Etta flew in a figure of eight around their heads. "One of the monkeys told me you'd entered the safari park's competition. I was hoping you'd win!"

Rachel and Kirsty shared a glance. "How did the monkeys know?" Rachel asked curiously.

Etta gave a laugh. "Monkeys are really nosy. They make it their business to know everything." She flew around their heads. "I have an extra prize for you. Would you like to come with me to Fairyland and see Sparkle Forest? It's a special place where all species of animals can live together."

"Yes, please!" the girls said. They knew they didn't need to worry about Mr and Mrs Walker missing them. Whenever they went to Fairyland, time stayed still in the real world. They would definitely be back in time to see the elephants.

Etta waved her wand before their faces, scattering fairy dust. She began to circle around them, flying faster and faster until her little wings made their hair lift and dance before their eyes. The girls shook their eyes clear and – there! – they were

floating above a place even more special than the safari park. They were as small as Etta, and pale, silvery wings poked out from between their shoulder blades.

Below them was a magical forest. Half of the trees were dusted in snow that looked like icing sugar. The other part of

the forest had trees with big, glossy leaves and vines hanging from their branches. Rachel and Kirsty had to rub their eyes. It was like looking at two halves of the world, brought together!

They drifted down into the heart of the forest, and Etta landed beside them. Little pink faces peered out from behind tree trunks and, one by one, three other fairies came to join them, tiptoeing through the long grass.

"Meet the rest of the Endangered Animals Fairies," Etta said, smiling at them. "This is Priya the Polar Bear Fairy." Priya gave a little shake of her white woollen gloves. "And this is Chelsea the Chimpanzee Fairy." Chelsea grinned and waved her fairy wings at them.

"And I'm Selma the Snow Leopard

Fairy!" said the last fairy, dancing through the air in delight. She came down to land beside Rachel and Kirsty.

Each of the fairies had a baby creature with her. They took it in turns to

introduce their magical friends. "This is my polar bear, Snowy," said Priya, rubbing her nose into Snowy's white fur.

"And say hello to Bobo," Chelsea said. "We call him Bouncy Bobo because he bounces around so much!" The chimpanzee leapt out of her arms and scrambled into a tree, leaping from branch to branch – bounce, bounce, bounce. "See?" They all burst out laughing.

"This is Strider," said Selma, stroking a hand down her snow leopard's fur. "She's called Strider

because …"

"She has such long legs!" Rachel said quickly.

Etta picked up her own baby creature – a small grey elephant with pink ears and feet that almost looked too big for his body. "This is Stampy," Etta said, pointing out his huge feet. "He trips over himself sometimes."

"Your baby animals are so cute," Kirsty said. "I wish I had one."

Etta shook her head. "It's only in Sparkle Forest that fairies and animals can live so close together. Back in your world, it's important that wild animals are allowed to live on their own."

"You're so lucky to live here," Kirsty said, gazing around. "I never thought

I'd say this, but you've brought us somewhere even more amazing than Trunk and Tail!"

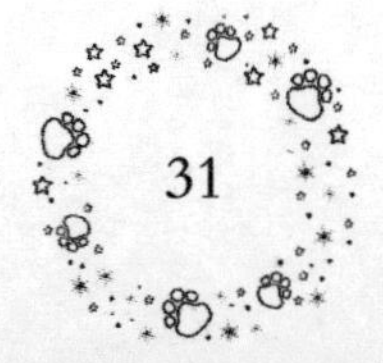

Chapter Three
Stop Thief!

All sorts of animals had followed the fairies out from the forest, and now they gathered in the glade. Butterflies with huge rainbow-coloured wings danced above their heads, and a tiger stretched out in the sun, nuzzling his nose up to a smiling polar bear.

"We wouldn't see polar bears in the safari park," Rachel said, her eyes wide.

"We're lucky here," Etta said. "All animals can survive in Sparkle Forest, even if they are endangered in the human world. That's why we must always keep the animals of Sparkle Forest safe."

"There are lots of other animals to see," said Selma. "Come and look." She led them deeper into the forest and they

saw lizards, frogs, a hairy orang-utan and a coal-black panther that padded behind a tree, its amber eyes glinting.

As they held their breath, waiting for the panther to come back out again, a hunched figure emerged from a hole in one of the tree trunks.

"Jack Frost!" Kirsty said. The Ice Lord was always causing trouble for the girls' fairy friends. One of his goblin servants cartwheeled across the forest floor

and two others leapt down from a tree branch. They laughed with delight.

"I've been looking for some new pets," Jack Frost said, his rasping voice echoing off the trees. "These lovely creatures are perfect for the zoo at my Ice Castle!"

The goblins darted between the trees and snatched the fairies' animal companions out of their arms. The magical creatures wriggled as hard as they could, but they weren't strong enough to escape.

"Put them down!" Etta said bravely. Stampy raised his trunk in the air and

made a miserable trumpeting sound. It was cruel to keep animals against their will, but Jack Frost didn't care about that. He blew a loud raspberry.

"Bring the animals back to the Ice Castle," he told his goblins. He waved a bony hand at them and blue light shot through the air. "Here's some magic to

make your journey quicker. I'll go ahead and make sure the zoo's cages are ready. I've got lots of stinky damp straw. Hee, hee!" Then he disappeared in another flash of blue lightning.

"Cages? That's awful!" Etta said. She placed her fists on her hips and her brow creased in a frown. "No animal should be treated like that."

Jack Frost's naughty helpers didn't seem to be in a rush to get to the Ice Castle. One of the goblins stroked the polar bear with a bony hand and another one was trying to count the baby cheetah's spots. The third goblin laughed with delight at the chimpanzee's cute pink face.

"We don't have to go back right away," another goblin said. "We could hide in the human world and have fun playing

with our new pets."

"You think these animals are toys, but they're not," Etta said angrily. "They're rare creatures and they need protecting."

But the goblins weren't listening. Their eyes lit up with delight as they

Chapter Four
Sweets for Stampy

"Where are they going now?" Etta asked.

Rachel and Kirsty shared a glance. "That's the way we arrived at Sparkle Forest. They're headed towards the safari park."

"We have to stop them!" said Etta. "Our animals shouldn't leave Sparkle Forest at all."

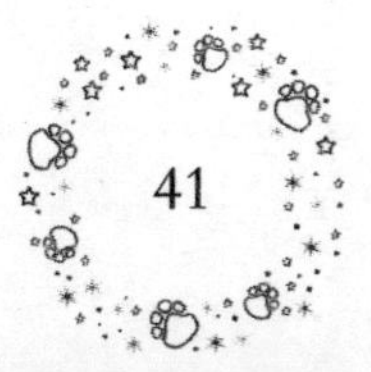

Rachel and Kirsty launched themselves into the air, bobbing up and down. They were so cross! "Don't worry, we'll help get them back," Rachel said.

"Definitely!" Kirsty agreed. She reached out a hand to Rachel and another one to Etta. Then Etta gave a wave of her wand and a cascade of sparkling fairy dust rained down over them, making Kirsty's nose tickle.

"Atchoo!"

She sneezed so hard that she squeezed her eyes tight shut. When she opened them again, she was standing by the elephant enclosure at Tail and Trunk Safari Park. She and Rachel were back to normal size.

The girls went to the edge of a muddy pool with a wooden sign beside it that read 'Elephant Bath'. But things didn't look right at all. The water had shrunk to the size of a puddle and the mud around the edges of the pool had dried hard, like a pie crust.

"There's no way an elephant could have a bath in that!" Kirsty said. She raised a hand to touch a tree branch and dry, brittle leaves rained down over her head. From the other side of the pond came a long, unhappy moan. It was the elephants, huddled beneath a bare tree. Stampy was with them. He had grown to

the size of a normal baby elephant. His little pink tongue poked out of his mouth as he panted. He looked thirsty.

"They don't have anything to eat or drink," Rachel said, looking around at all the trees and bushes. They were dry and brittle, their branches drooping and their leaves in little piles on the ground. "I don't understand what's happening."

"I do," said Etta, flying around a tree trunk. "The goblins shouldn't have come here. Now that they have, it's spoiling the

safari park."

"This is what happens when you mess about with nature," Kirsty said.

There was a movement behind one of the bare trees. Kirsty recognised the green face and huge feet of a goblin. He thought the girls couldn't see him hiding behind the tree, but there were no leaves to camouflage him.

He crept out and reached a long, bony hand into a red-and-white striped paper bag.

"It looks as though he's visited the safari park's gift shop," Rachel said. They'd passed

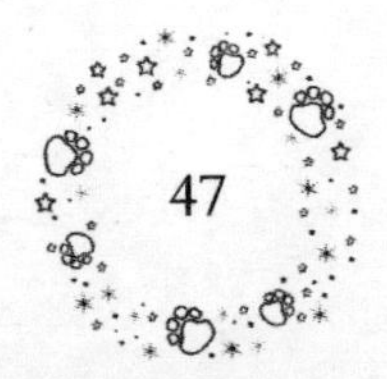

the shop on their drive into the park and she'd seen the rows of sweet jars in the window.

The goblin began to throw sweeties

towards the elephants. "Here! Have a gobstopper!" they heard him say.

"He's feeding them sweets!" Etta said, gasping.

Kirsty folded her arms. "The goblins have spoilt the park by coming here and now this one is giving the elephants

sugary foods!"

Rachel frowned. "It's not good for them," she said. "We have to stop him."

Kirsty and Rachel raced around the edge of the pond, towards the elephants. Etta flew across the water. Maybe they could scare the goblin off.

But the sun was dipping in the sky. Soon, Mr and Mrs Walker would be calling them for their supper. The girls needed to work fast!

Chapter Five
Race You!

When they arrived on the other side of the pond, they could see that the elephants were bent over something. It was the pile of sweets that the goblin had scattered in the grass.

Rachel knew from her school project that elephants needed to eat other things to survive. Things like leaves and vegetables, fruit ... and tree bark! That

gave Rachel an idea. As Etta and Kirsty tried to shoo the goblin away, she picked up a piece of tree bark from where it had fallen on the ground.

"Come here, Stampy!" she said in a soft voice, holding out the bark. "Are you hungry?" Etta saw what she was doing and came to dance in the air above Rachel's shoulder. The baby elephant's

eyes lit up to see its friend. Stampy left the other elephants to reach out his trunk for the tasty snack. Etta was nearly reunited with her friend, when the goblin pushed past Kirsty to race over.

"Stop that!" he said. "Stampy belongs to me."

"Wild animals don't belong to anyone," Rachel told him. The goblin wasn't listening. He tried to throw his arms around Stampy's neck, but the elephant wriggled free and ran off towards the Walkers' cabin. He was getting faster and faster. The friends had to stop him! No one could know

that there was a magical elephant in Tail and Trunk Safari Park.

They chased after him. Stampy swerved around a fallen tree trunk and – whoops! – he stumbled over his own big feet. Before he could start running again, Rachel caught up with him. Stampy looked around, as though he suddenly

realised he was no longer with his friends by the Elephant Bath. He started trembling! Normally, Rachel would never touch a wild animal, but the little elephant needed comforting.

She stroked the soft grey skin of Stampy's trunk and rested her cheek against his face. "There, there," she said

softly, over and over. Kirsty came around the other side and did the same. Etta flew in the air above Stampy's head, using her wings to cool him down after his run.

Stampy began to look happier and they led him back to the pond. He trotted happily between them. He tried to reach his trunk out to the pond, but the water had disappeared down to almost nothing.

"Etta, can you use your magic again?" Rachel called up. Etta didn't hesitate. She flew around the Elephant Bath and touched the tip of her wand to the trees and the surface of the water, saying a spell as she worked:

Water bright and leaves so green
A pretty picture to be seen.
Food and water's what we need
To help these creatures drink and feed.

Leaves curled out of the branches and the pond's water turned blue and rippled in waves. The elephants crowded round, eating and drinking. Stampy nibbled a leaf and then dipped his trunk in the water, his eyes closing in delight as he drank.

There was the sound of a miserable

snarl from behind them. The goblin was watching them unhappily.

"All those empty cages in the zoo at the Ice Castle," he said. "Jack Frost won't be happy."

"Did you really want to see Stampy in a cage?" asked Rachel gently. The baby elephant was playing happily with Etta, chasing her around the tree trunk. "Just look! These creatures are meant to be free."

As they watched, Etta came down and landed between Stampy's soft, grey ears.

The goblin gave a wonky smile as he watched them.

"Are you going to take him back to Sparkle Forest?" he asked.

"Yes," Etta said. "Why don't you come back, too? You can visit the glade, as long as you promise to let Stampy and the other animals have their freedom."

"I promise," the goblin said.

"Then we can all go home," Etta said.

She gazed over towards Rachel and Kirsty. "Thank you so much for your help."

The two girls waved. "We couldn't have fed and watered the elephants without your magic," Kirsty told their fairy friend.

Etta gave a smile, then circled her wand through the air. In a cloud of sparkles, Etta, Stampy and the goblin disappeared.

Chapter Six
Hot Dogs All Round

Rachel and Kirsty walked back towards their cabin. Mrs Walker was carrying a plate piled up with hot dogs and Mr Walker was pouring lemonade from a tall glass jar. Ahmed was with them, eating a huge hot dog.

"Do you want to go and see the elephants after we've eaten?" he said through a mouthful of hot dog.

The girls shared a secret smile. "Will there be any nosy monkeys there?" Kirsty asked, remembering that a monkey had told Etta they were in the safari park. She reached for a couple of hot dogs and passed one to Rachel.

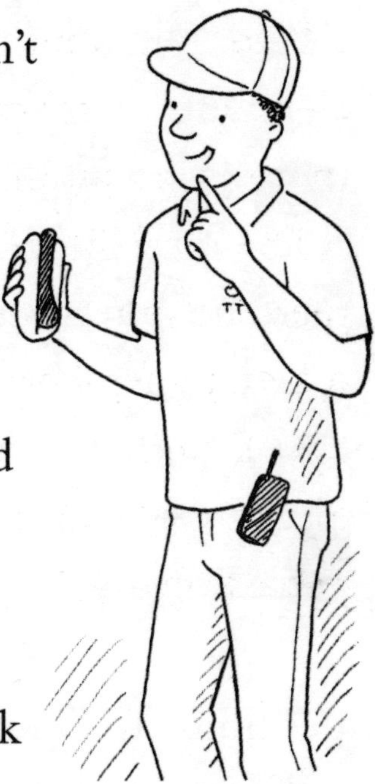

Ahmed frowned. "I don't think so," he said. "I've never seen a monkey at the Elephant Bath." His face lit up. "But we could go to the monkey enclosure afterwards, and then visit the meerkats. Did you know that meerkats sunbathe and use their tummies to soak up heat from the sun?"

"Fascinating!" Rachel said. Ahmed loved his aninal facts.

Rachel pulled Kirsty to one side so that she could whisper. "I'd love to see the meerkats," she said, "but there's still a snow leopard, chimpanzee and polar cub in the safari park. We need to help them

get home to Sparkle Forest."

Kirsty nodded. "Let's see if we can stay a few more days at the safari park," she whispered. "It is half term, after all."

"I have an idea," Rachel said. Then she turned to her mum and dad, who were clearing away the plates. "Could Kirsty and I stay here a few more days, to help out Ahmed around the park?"

Mr and Mrs Walker looked at each other and grinned. "That's a wonderful idea," Mrs Walker said. "Just let us phone Kirsty's parents to check." The two of them disappeared into the cabin.

Ahmed was climbing back into his tiger-striped truck. Rachel and Kirsty ran after him.

"Ahmed, would you like if we stayed a few more days to give you some extra help around the park?" they asked, jumping up and down on the spot.

Ahmed frowned, pretending to think. "That would be … a wonderful idea! I'll have a think what I might need help with," he said, before driving off.

Rachel and Kirsty put their arms

around each other's shoulders as they waved the park manager off. There were three more magical baby animals to save at Tail and Trunk Safari Park. They'd better get a good night's sleep.

The End

Now it's time for Kirsty and Rachel to help ...

Priya the Polar Bear Fairy

Read on for a sneak peek ...

Kirsty Tate was dreaming.

In the dream, her best friend Rachel Walker was calling her name, but every time Kirsty tried to reply, an elephant trumpeted loudly.

"Kirsty!" called Rachel again.

This time, the elephant's trumpeting was so loud that it woke Kirsty up. She smiled and sat up in bed. Rachel was sitting up in the bed on the other side of the room. There really was an elephant trumpeting in the distance, and now Kirsty remembered why. She and Rachel were staying at the Tail and Trunk Safari

Park, just outside Wetherbury Village. They had won a picture competition, and the prize was a stay at the safari park.

"Ahmed said he'd pick us up first thing this morning," said Kirsty, swinging her legs out of bed. "I wonder which animals we'll be visiting first today."

Ahmed was their tour guide. He had already shown them lots of wonderful animals at the safari park, and he had promised that there were plenty more to see.

"And I wonder which of our fairy friends we'll be seeing today," Rachel added, peeping out of the window. "The Endangered Animals Fairies really need our help, Kirsty."

The girls got dressed, chatting about the magical adventure they had shared the day before. Etta the Elephant Fairy had taken them to Sparkle Forest in Fairyland, where they had met the Endangered Animals Fairies. The fairies looked after animal habitats in the human world, and kept endangered species safe in Fairyland. But while Rachel and Kirsty were in Sparkle Forest, Jack Frost had appeared with his goblins and kidnapped the fairies' magical companions. To make things even more complicated, the goblins had disobeyed their master and taken the enchanted animals off to the human world.

"We can't let Jack Frost put the animals in cages for his own private zoo," said Kirsty in a determined voice.

"We just have to find those goblins before Jack Frost does," Rachel added. "Or animal habitats will be spoiled and rare animals will be in more danger than ever."

They were interrupted by Mrs Walker popping her head around the door.

"Morning!" she said. "Oh good, you're up. Ahmed will be here soon."

"We can't wait," said Kirsty.

"I spoke to your parents last night," Mrs Walker added, smiling at Kirsty. "They're happy for you to stay with us at the safari park for two more days."

Rachel and Kirsty shared a happy hug. Just then, they heard a jeep pull up outside.

"Ahmed's here," called Mr Walker.

The girls ran outside, picking up some toast on the way. Ahmed was sitting in his tiger-striped jeep, and the engine was purring.

"Good morning," he said, flashing them a broad smile. "I hear that you're going to be around for a few more days. Fantastic!"

"Where are we going first?" asked Rachel excitedly.

"I thought I'd take you to visit the polar bears this morning," said Ahmed.

"Oh yes, I'd love that," said Kirsty as she and Rachel put on their seatbelts.

The jeep rumbled towards the heart of the safari park. Even though it was early, the sun was already extremely hot. Many animals were still sheltering inside their enclosures.

"I think polar bears are beautiful," said Rachel, in between bites of toast. "I love their white fur."

"Actually, polar bears have transparent fur," said Ahmed. "And did you know that their skin is black?"

"No, we didn't," said Rachel and Kirsty,

sharing a smile.

They had already learned that Ahmed was full of amazing facts about all their favourite animals.

"The polar bear keeper, Elkie, will be able to tell you lots more," he said. "She's been here ever since the bears arrived, and there's nothing she doesn't know about them."

A few minutes later, Ahmed stopped the jeep on one of the park's wide paths.

"We have to go the rest of the way on foot," he said.

He led Rachel and Kirsty along a narrow walkway that went all around the polar bear enclosure. Two adult polar bears and a wriggly little cub were lying on a rock beside a pool. A low archway was cut into the rock behind them. The three polar bears were panting in the morning sunshine.

"The adults are called Charlie and Matilda, after two of Elkie's favourite books," said Ahmed. "And the baby is called James."

Rachel and Kirsty smiled. They loved those books too.

"Don't they miss having ice and snow?" Kirsty asked. "They look a bit hot."

"Polar bears are very adaptable," said Ahmed. "But actually, we've made sure they have ice too. That archway in the rock leads to a special ice-cave habitat. I'm not sure why they're not in there on this hot morning, actually. Come on, I'll show you."

Ahmed led the girls around the walkway and down some steps.

"We have a viewing gallery so visitors

can see the polar bears enjoying their natural habitat," he explained. "It's a shame it has to be inside, but that's the only way for us to keep it cold enough."

They reached the bottom of the steps and found themselves in a large underground chamber.

Calling all parents, carers and teachers!
The Rainbow Magic fairies are here to help your child enter the magical world of reading. Whatever reading stage they are at, there's a Rainbow Magic book for everyone!
Here is Lydia the Reading Fairy's guide to supporting your child's journey at all levels.

1

Starting Out

Our Rainbow Magic Beginner Readers are perfect for first-time readers who are just beginning to develop reading skills and confidence. Approved by teachers, they contain a full range of educational levelling, as well as lively full-colour illustrations.

2

Developing Readers

Rainbow Magic Early Readers contain longer stories and wider vocabulary for building stamina and growing confidence. These are adaptations of our most popular Rainbow Magic stories, specially developed for younger readers in conjunction with an Early Years reading consultant, with full-colour illustrations.

3

Going Solo

The Rainbow Magic chapter books – a mixture of series and one-off specials – contain accessible writing to encourage your child to venture into reading independently. These highly collectible and much-loved magical stories inspire a love of reading to last a lifetime.

www.rainbowmagicbooks.co.uk

"Rainbow Magic got my daughter reading chapter books. Great sparkly covers, cute fairies and traditional stories full of magic that she found impossible to put down" – Mother of Edie (6 years)

"Florence LOVES the Rainbow Magic books. She really enjoys reading now" – Mother of Florence (6 years)

The Rainbow Magic Reading Challenge

Well done, fairy friend – you have completed the book!
This book was worth 5 points.

See how far you have climbed on the **Reading Rainbow** opposite.

The more books you read, the more points you will get, and the closer you will be to becoming a Fairy Princess!

How to get your Reading Rainbow

1. Cut out the coin below
2. Go to the Rainbow Magic website
3. Download and print out your poster
4. Add your coin and climb up the Reading Rainbow!

There's all this and lots more at
www.rainbowmagicbooks.co.uk

You'll find activities, competitions, stories, a special newsletter and complete profiles of all the Rainbow Magic fairies. Find a fairy with your name!